Dictatorship Diaries

America Literature 20th century, Volume 1

MICHAEL SMITH

Published by Graywolf Press, 2024.

This is a work of fiction. Similarities to real people, places, or events are entirely coincidental.

DICTATORSHIP DIARIES

First edition. May 14, 2024.

ISBN: 979-8224006922

Written by MICHAEL SMITH.

Table of Contents

For those who endured the darkness of dictatorship,

And for those who tirelessly strive for the light of democracy,

This book is dedicated to the victims, the survivors, and the seekers of truth and justice.

May their stories inspire us to remember, to resist, and to rebuild.

Chapter 1: Introduction

In the vast tapestry of Latin American history, the early 20th century was a period of profound transformation, marked by seismic shifts in political, economic, and social landscapes. This chapter serves as a foundational exploration of the conditions that paved the way for the rise of authoritarian regimes across the region. We delve into the complex interplay of historical events, socio-political dynamics, and external influences that catalyzed the emergence of dictatorships in Latin America. Furthermore, we outline the overarching objectives of this book, aiming to dissect and analyze the commonalities, differences, and enduring legacies of authoritarian rule in the region.

Setting the Stage: Overview of Latin America in the Early 20th Century

At the turn of the 20th century, Latin America found itself at a crossroads, grappling with the legacies of colonialism, the challenges of modernization, and the complexities of global geopolitics. Emerging from centuries of Spanish and Portuguese colonial rule, newly independent nations sought to define their identities and chart their destinies in an increasingly interconnected world.

The early 1900s witnessed a wave of nationalist fervor and political upheaval, as Latin American societies grappled with the tensions between tradition and modernity, rural and urban, indigenous and mestizo. Industrialization and urbanization fueled rapid demographic shifts, as rural migrants flocked to burgeoning cities in search of economic opportunities. However, these urban centers often became hotbeds of social unrest, characterized by stark inequalities, overcrowded slums, and labor exploitation.

Meanwhile, the specter of foreign intervention loomed large over the region, as imperial powers vied for influence and resources in Latin America. The United States, in particular, wielded considerable economic and political clout, intervening militarily in countries like Mexico, Nicaragua, and Haiti to safeguard its strategic interests. The imposition of unequal treaties, such as the Panama Canal Zone and the Platt Amendment in Cuba, underscored the asymmetrical power dynamics between Latin America and its northern neighbor.

Against this backdrop of instability and uncertainty, populist leaders and military strongmen emerged as champions of order and stability, promising to restore national greatness and protect the interests of the ruling elites. These authoritarian figures exploited widespread disillusionment with democratic institutions, scapegoating political opponents, ethnic minorities, and marginalized groups to consolidate their grip on power.

Rise of Authoritarianism: Socio-Political Factors Leading to the Emergence of Dictatorships

The rise of authoritarian regimes in Latin America was not a monolithic phenomenon but rather a multifaceted process shaped by a confluence of internal and external factors. Economic volatility, social dislocation, and political instability created fertile ground for authoritarian leaders to exploit popular grievances and entrench themselves in power.

Economic factors played a pivotal role in fueling the ascent of authoritarianism. Throughout the early 20th century, Latin America experienced cycles of boom and bust, as export-oriented economies fluctuated in response to global market conditions. Dependence on primary commodities, such as coffee, sugar, and minerals, left many countries vulnerable to external shocks, exacerbating poverty, inequality, and social unrest.

Moreover, the concentration of landownership and wealth in the hands of a small elite perpetuated socio-economic disparities, deepening class divisions and exacerbating rural poverty. Peasant uprisings and labor strikes became increasingly common, as agrarian workers and urban laborers demanded land reform, labor rights, and greater economic justice.

In response to these challenges, traditional political institutions struggled to maintain legitimacy and effectiveness, paving the way for populist demagogues and military strongmen to seize power through extra-constitutional means. Weak rule of law, endemic corruption, and clientelistic networks further eroded public trust in democratic governance, creating openings for authoritarian leaders to exploit.

External factors also played a significant role in shaping the trajectory of authoritarianism in Latin America. The United States, as the dominant power in the Western Hemisphere, wielded considerable influence through its economic, diplomatic, and military interventions. The doctrine of "Manifest Destiny" and the Monroe Doctrine justified American interventionism, framing Latin America as a sphere of influence to be managed and controlled.

During the Cold War era, the specter of communism loomed large over Latin America, as the United States sought to contain the spread of leftist movements and revolutionary ideologies. The fear of communist infiltration provided a pretext for supporting repressive regimes and undermining democratic governments perceived as sympathetic to socialist causes. The legacy of U.S. interventionism in countries like Guatemala, Chile, and Nicaragua continues to reverberate through the region to this day, fueling anti-American sentiment and fostering distrust of external powers.

Objectives of the Book: Understanding the Commonalities, Differences, and Legacies of Dictatorships in Latin America

Against this backdrop of historical context and socio-political dynamics, this book seeks to unravel the complexities of authoritarian rule in Latin America, shedding light on the commonalities, differences, and enduring legacies of dictatorship across the region. Through a comparative analysis of case studies spanning the 20th century, we aim to elucidate the underlying patterns and dynamics that shaped the rise, consolidation, and downfall of authoritarian regimes in Latin America.

Key objectives of the book include:

1. Historical Contextualization: Providing a nuanced understanding of the historical, economic, and social factors that contributed to the emergence of dictatorship in Latin America, contextualizing each case study within its broader historical framework.

2. Comparative Analysis: Identifying commonalities and differences among authoritarian regimes in terms of their ideological underpinnings, modes of governance, and strategies of repression, drawing parallels and contrasts between different countries and historical periods.

3. Impact Assessment : Assessing the social, economic, and political impact of authoritarian rule on Latin American societies, examining the legacies of dictatorship in terms of democratic governance, human rights, and political culture.

4. Memory and Reconciliation: Exploring efforts to commemorate the victims of dictatorship, promote truth and reconciliation, and confront the legacy of state-sponsored violence and repression, highlighting the ongoing struggles for justice and accountability in post-authoritarian societies.

By examining the rise and fall of authoritarian regimes in Latin America through a multidisciplinary lens, this book aims to deepen our understanding of the complexities of power, ideology, and resistance in the region's tumultuous history. Through rigorous analysis and critical reflection, we endeavor to illuminate the enduring legacy of dictatorship and its implications for the quest for democracy, justice, and human rights in Latin America and beyond.

Chapter 2: The Roots of Dictatorship

In understanding the emergence of dictatorship in Latin America, it is essential to trace its roots back to the historical, economic, and social conditions that laid the groundwork for authoritarian rule. This chapter delves into the deep-seated factors that contributed to the rise of dictatorship in the region, examining the enduring legacies of colonialism, the persistence of economic instability and social inequality, and the pivotal role of populist leaders and military interventions in shaping the trajectory of Latin American politics.

Historical Background: Colonial Legacies and Early Independence Struggles

The roots of dictatorship in Latin America can be traced back to the legacies of colonialism and the tumultuous process of independence from Spanish and Portuguese rule. For centuries, Latin America served as a lucrative source of wealth for European colonial powers, with the extraction of precious metals, cash crops, and slave labor fueling the growth of global empires. The hierarchical social structures established by colonial regimes entrenched divisions based on race, class, and ethnicity, laying the foundation for enduring patterns of inequality and exclusion.

The struggle for independence in the early 19th century marked a watershed moment in Latin American history, as colonies across the region sought to break free from imperial domination and assert their sovereignty. However, the transition from colonial rule to independent nation-states was fraught with challenges, as competing factions vied for power and influence in the vacuum left by departing colonial authorities.

The legacy of colonialism cast a long shadow over the newly independent nations of Latin America, shaping their political institutions, social hierarchies, and economic structures. The concentration of landownership in the hands of a privileged few, inherited from the colonial era, perpetuated patterns of inequality and exploitation, as wealthy landowners wielded disproportionate influence over politics and society.

Economic Instability and Social Inequality

Throughout the 19th and early 20th centuries, Latin America grappled with persistent economic instability, driven by a volatile combination of external shocks, internal conflicts, and structural vulnerabilities. The region's dependence on primary commodities, such as minerals, agricultural products, and raw materials, left it vulnerable to fluctuations in global market prices, exposing countries to the whims of international capitalism.

Moreover, the legacy of colonialism perpetuated patterns of social inequality, as indigenous communities, Afro-descendant populations, and rural peasants were marginalized and excluded from the benefits of economic development. Land concentration, unequal access to education and healthcare, and discriminatory labor practices entrenched disparities along racial, ethnic, and class lines, fostering social tensions and unrest.

The emergence of an urban proletariat, fueled by rural-to-urban migration and industrialization, posed new challenges to the established order, as labor movements and socialist ideologies gained traction among urban workers. However, the entrenched power structures of the landed elite and the military oligarchy often resisted efforts at reform, using violence and repression to maintain their privileged position.

Rise of Populist Leaders and Military Interventions

Amidst growing discontent and social unrest, populist leaders and military strongmen emerged as messianic figures promising to restore order, stability, and national greatness. These charismatic leaders capitalized on popular grievances, exploiting the rhetoric of nationalism, anti-imperialism, and social justice to mobilize support among the masses.

Populist leaders like Juan Perón in Argentina, Getúlio Vargas in Brazil, and Lázaro Cárdenas in Mexico tapped into a potent mix of nationalism, populism, and corporatism to consolidate power and implement sweeping reforms. Their charismatic leadership style and populist policies endeared them to the working class and marginalized sectors of society, while simultaneously alienating traditional elites and conservative forces.

Military interventions became a recurrent feature of Latin American politics, as armed forces often saw themselves as the guardians of order and stability in times of crisis. The military, imbued with a sense of mission and duty, intervened in politics to restore law and order, suppress dissent, and safeguard the interests of the ruling elite. However, the militarization of politics also posed a grave threat to democratic governance, as military regimes often ruled with an iron fist, curtailing civil liberties, and human rights in the name of national security.

Conclusion

In tracing the roots of dictatorship in Latin America, it becomes evident that authoritarian rule was not merely a deviation from democratic norms but rather a manifestation of deep-seated historical, economic, and social forces. The legacy of colonialism, the persistence of economic instability and social inequality, and the rise of populist leaders and military interventions all contributed to the emergence of dictatorship as a recurrent phenomenon in the region's history.

By understanding the historical roots of dictatorship in Latin America, we gain valuable insights into the complex interplay of power, ideology, and resistance that shaped the trajectory of the region's politics. Moving forward, it is essential to confront these historical legacies and address the root causes of authoritarianism, fostering inclusive and democratic institutions that uphold the principles of justice, equality, and human rights for all citizens.

Chapter 3: The Machado Era: Cuba, 1925-1933

The Machado era in Cuba, spanning from 1925 to 1933, stands as a pivotal chapter in the island nation's history, marked by the rise of authoritarianism under the leadership of President Gerardo Machado. This chapter delves into the complex dynamics of the Machado regime, examining Fulgencio Batista's ascent to power, the widespread repression and censorship that characterized the era, and the economic policies and foreign relations that defined Cuba's trajectory during this turbulent period.

Fulgencio Batista's Rise to Power

The Machado era began in 1925 when Gerardo Machado assumed the presidency of Cuba, following a period of political instability and economic turmoil. Machado, a former army general, promised to bring order and prosperity to the island, presenting himself as a champion of modernization and progress. However, Machado's regime quickly descended into authoritarianism, as he consolidated power through a combination of electoral fraud, repression, and manipulation of the political system.

At the heart of Machado's regime was his close ally and chief enforcer, Fulgencio Batista, a charismatic army sergeant who rose to prominence as the head of the feared secret police, known as the "Bureau of Investigation and Repression" (BIR). Batista's loyalty to Machado, coupled with his ruthlessness and cunning, made him indispensable to the regime's survival, as he ruthlessly suppressed dissent and eliminated political opponents to maintain Machado's grip on power.

Batista's rise to prominence within the Machado regime was swift and meteoric, as he exploited his position as head of the BIR to amass wealth and influence, using intimidation and violence to quash any challenge to Machado's authority. Through a combination of coercion and manipulation, Batista emerged as the de facto ruler of Cuba, wielding unchecked power over the island's political, economic, and social affairs.

Repression and Censorship Under the Machado Regime

The Machado era was characterized by widespread repression and censorship, as the regime sought to silence dissent and stifle opposition to its authoritarian rule. Political opponents, labor activists, and journalists who dared to criticize the government were subject to harassment, intimidation, and arrest, as Machado and Batista cracked down on perceived threats to their authority.

The regime's use of censorship was particularly draconian, as newspapers, radio stations, and other media outlets were tightly controlled by the government, with any dissenting voices swiftly silenced or suppressed. Independent journalists and intellectuals who dared to speak out against Machado's regime faced harassment, exile, or imprisonment, as the regime sought to maintain a stranglehold on the flow of information and control the narrative of Cuban politics.

Labor unions and social movements were also targeted by the regime, as Machado and Batista viewed organized labor as a potential threat to their authority. Strikes and protests were brutally suppressed by the security forces, with workers subjected to violence, intimidation, and imprisonment for daring to demand better wages, working conditions, and political rights.

Economic Policies and Foreign Relations

Despite the repression and authoritarianism that characterized the Machado era, the regime pursued ambitious economic policies aimed at modernizing and industrializing the Cuban economy. Machado implemented a series of infrastructure projects, including the construction of highways, ports, and public buildings, in a bid to stimulate economic growth and attract foreign investment.

However, these ambitious development projects came at a steep cost, as Machado's government borrowed heavily from foreign creditors to finance its ambitious agenda, leading to soaring levels of debt and economic instability. Moreover, the benefits of economic growth were unevenly distributed, with the vast majority of Cubans seeing little improvement in their living standards, while the ruling elite and foreign investors reaped the rewards of economic development.

Foreign relations during the Machado era were characterized by a delicate balancing act between the United States, Cuba's powerful northern neighbor, and other regional powers in Latin America. Machado sought to maintain cordial relations with the United States, Cuba's largest trading partner and source of investment, while also cultivating ties with other Latin American countries in order to bolster Cuba's standing in the region.

However, Machado's authoritarian rule and repressive tactics strained relations with the United States, as American officials grew increasingly concerned about the erosion of democracy and human rights in Cuba. The outbreak of the Great Depression in 1929 further exacerbated tensions, as Cuba's economy faltered and social unrest threatened to destabilize the island.

Conclusion

The Machado era in Cuba was a period of intense repression, censorship, and economic instability, as President Gerardo Machado and his chief enforcer, Fulgencio Batista, ruthlessly clung to power through a combination of coercion, manipulation, and violence. Despite their promises of progress and prosperity, Machado's regime failed to address the underlying social and economic inequalities that plagued Cuban society, leading to widespread discontent and opposition.

The legacy of the Machado era continues to reverberate through Cuban history, serving as a cautionary tale of the dangers of unchecked authoritarianism and the perils of political repression. The rise of Fulgencio Batista within the Machado regime foreshadowed his own ascent to power as dictator of Cuba in the years to come, as he would go on to rule the island with an iron fist for nearly two decades before being overthrown by the Cuban Revolution in 1959.

In examining the Machado era, we gain valuable insights into the complex dynamics of power, ideology, and resistance that shaped Cuban politics during this tumultuous period. Moving forward, it is essential to confront the legacies of authoritarianism and repression in Cuba, fostering a culture of democracy, human rights, and accountability that honors the memory of those who suffered under the yoke of dictatorship.

Chapter 4: The Vargas Years: Brazil, 1930-1945

The period from 1930 to 1945, known as the Vargas Years, represents a transformative chapter in Brazilian history, marked by the rise to power of Getúlio Vargas and the implementation of his authoritarian regime. This chapter explores Vargas's ascent to power, the establishment of Estado Novo (New State), characterized by censorship, nationalism, and corporatism, and the enduring legacy of Vargas's rule in Brazilian politics.

Getúlio Vargas's Ascent to Power

Getúlio Vargas's rise to power in Brazil was precipitated by a period of political instability and economic turmoil, as the country grappled with the consequences of the Great Depression and the collapse of the coffee-dominated economy. Vargas, a charismatic politician from the southern state of Rio Grande do Sul, emerged as a populist leader capable of mobilizing support across regional and ideological divides.

In 1930, amid widespread dissatisfaction with the ruling oligarchies and allegations of electoral fraud, Vargas orchestrated a coup d'état, overthrowing President Washington Luís and seizing power for himself. Presented as a temporary measure to restore order and stability, Vargas's provisional government quickly consolidated power, sidelining political opponents and centralizing authority under his leadership.

Vargas's initial tenure as president, known as the Provisional Government (1930-1934), was characterized by a series of reforms aimed at modernizing Brazil's economy and society. He implemented labor laws, established social welfare programs, and promoted industrialization, positioning himself as a champion of the working class and the downtrodden.

However, Vargas's populist rhetoric masked his authoritarian tendencies, as he sought to consolidate power and establish his dominance over Brazilian politics. In 1934, he orchestrated the drafting of a new constitution, which extended his term as president and expanded executive authority, laying the groundwork for the establishment of Estado Novo.

Implementation of Estado Novo: Censorship, Nationalism, and Corporatism

In 1937, Vargas officially inaugurated Estado Novo, a corporatist and authoritarian regime characterized by censorship, nationalism, and the suppression of political opposition. Modeled after European fascist regimes, Estado Novo sought to centralize power in the hands of the state, suppress dissent, and promote a vision of national unity and discipline.

Under Estado Novo, Vargas exercised near-total control over the political, economic, and cultural life of Brazil, ruling by decree and suppressing political opposition through censorship, intimidation, and repression. The regime established a pervasive system of censorship, controlling the press, radio, and other media outlets to ensure that only pro-government propaganda was disseminated to the public.

Nationalism was a central tenet of Estado Novo ideology, as Vargas sought to foster a sense of Brazilian identity and pride in the face of perceived foreign threats and influences. The regime promoted symbols of national unity, such as the Brazilian flag and anthem, while demonizing perceived enemies, including communists, liberals, and foreign powers.

Corporatism was another key feature of Estado Novo, as Vargas sought to co-opt and control organized interest groups, including labor unions, business associations, and professional organizations. These corporatist structures served to channel social and economic grievances into channels approved by the state, while suppressing independent forms of political expression and organization.

Legacy of Vargas's Rule in Brazilian Politics

The legacy of the Vargas years continues to loom large in Brazilian politics and society, shaping the country's political trajectory and identity to this day. Despite his authoritarian methods and repressive tactics, Vargas is often remembered as a transformative figure who modernized Brazil's economy, expanded social welfare programs, and promoted a sense of national unity and identity.

Vargas's populist legacy endures in Brazilian politics, as successive generations of politicians have sought to emulate his blend of authoritarianism and populism, promising to address the country's deep-seated inequalities and social injustices. However, Vargas's authoritarian tendencies also cast a long shadow over Brazilian democracy, as his legacy of centralized power and suppression of political opposition continue to influence the country's political culture and institutions.

In conclusion, the Vargas years represent a complex and contradictory chapter in Brazilian history, marked by the tension between authoritarianism and populism, nationalism and democracy. While Vargas's regime succeeded in modernizing Brazil's economy and promoting a sense of national identity, it also entrenched patterns of political repression and authoritarian rule that continue to shape the country's political landscape to this day. As Brazil grapples with the challenges of democratic governance and social justice in the 21st century, the legacy of the Vargas years remains a central point of reference in the country's ongoing quest for progress and development.

Chapter 5: The Trujillo Regime: Dominican Republic, 1930-1961

The Trujillo regime, spanning from 1930 to 1961, represents one of the darkest chapters in Dominican history, characterized by the ruthless dictatorship of Rafael Trujillo. This chapter explores Trujillo's consolidation of power, the establishment of a cult of personality and totalitarian control, and the profound impact of his regime on Dominican society and economy.

Rafael Trujillo's Consolidation of Power

Rafael Trujillo's ascent to power in the Dominican Republic was marked by political opportunism, violence, and manipulation. In 1930, Trujillo seized control of the government in a military coup, overthrowing President Horacio Vásquez and establishing himself as the undisputed ruler of the country. Trujillo's authoritarian regime quickly consolidated power, as he purged political opponents, co-opted key institutions, and established a pervasive system of surveillance and control.

Trujillo's rise to power was facilitated by his background as a military officer and his skillful manipulation of Dominican politics. He cultivated alliances with the military, business elite, and foreign powers, while ruthlessly eliminating rivals and dissenters through intimidation, violence, and assassination. Through a combination of coercion and patronage, Trujillo established a network of loyal supporters and collaborators, ensuring his grip on power remained unchallenged.

Once in power, Trujillo set about centralizing authority and suppressing opposition through a combination of propaganda, censorship, and repression. He cultivated a cult of personality, portraying himself as the savior of the nation and the embodiment of Dominican identity and pride. His image adorned public spaces, schools, and government buildings, while his regime controlled the flow of information and manipulated public opinion to maintain his popularity and legitimacy.

Cult of Personality and Totalitarian Control

Central to Trujillo's rule was the establishment of a cult of personality, which sought to deify him as the "Benefactor" and "Father of the New Dominican Republic." Trujillo's regime propagated an idealized image of the dictator as a visionary leader and national hero, while suppressing dissent and promoting loyalty through a combination of coercion and propaganda.

The cult of personality extended into every aspect of Dominican life, permeating education, culture, and religion. Schools were required to teach students about Trujillo's achievements and virtues, while artists and intellectuals were coerced into producing works that glorified the dictator and his regime. The Catholic Church, traditionally a source of moral authority and resistance, was co-opted by Trujillo, as the regime cultivated close ties with the clergy and promoted a brand of nationalism infused with religious symbolism.

Totalitarian control under Trujillo was enforced through a pervasive system of surveillance, censorship, and repression. The regime maintained a vast network of informants and secret police, monitoring the activities of perceived enemies and dissenters. Political opposition was brutally suppressed, with dissidents subjected to arbitrary arrest, torture, and imprisonment in notorious prisons such as La 40 and La Cuarenta.

Impact on Dominican Society and Economy

The Trujillo regime left an indelible mark on Dominican society and economy, shaping the country's trajectory for decades to come. Under Trujillo's rule, the Dominican Republic experienced rapid economic development, fueled by foreign investment, infrastructure projects, and industrialization. However, this development was unevenly distributed, benefiting the ruling elite and foreign investors at the expense of the majority of the population.

Trujillo's regime also exacerbated existing social inequalities, as political patronage and corruption enriched a small elite while leaving the majority of Dominicans mired in poverty and deprivation. The regime's policies of forced labor and land expropriation further marginalized rural peasants, displacing communities and destroying traditional ways of life.

Moreover, Trujillo's regime fostered a culture of fear and distrust, as pervasive surveillance and repression stifled dissent and suppressed political opposition. The regime's brutality and impunity created a climate of terror, as Dominicans lived in constant fear of arbitrary arrest, torture, and disappearance at the hands of the regime's security forces.

Conclusion

The Trujillo regime in the Dominican Republic represents a dark chapter in Latin American history, characterized by the ruthless dictatorship of Rafael Trujillo and the pervasive cult of personality and totalitarian control that he established. Trujillo's consolidation of power, manipulation of Dominican politics, and ruthless suppression of dissent left an indelible mark on Dominican society and economy, shaping the country's trajectory for decades to come.

As the Dominican Republic grapples with the legacy of the Trujillo regime, it is essential to confront the past and seek justice for the countless victims of dictatorship. By acknowledging the atrocities committed under Trujillo's rule and promoting a culture of democracy, human rights, and accountability, the Dominican Republic can honor the memory of those who suffered and ensure that such horrors are never repeated.

Chapter 6: Perónism in Argentina: 1946-1955

Perónism in Argentina represents one of the most significant and controversial chapters in the country's political history. Spanning from 1946 to 1955, the era of Juan Perón's rule and the rise of Peronism reshaped Argentine politics, society, and economy. This chapter explores Juan Perón's rise to power and his implementation of populist policies, the pivotal role of Eva Perón in shaping Peronist Argentina, and the enduring legacy of Perónism in Argentine politics.

Juan Perón's Rise to Power and Populist Policies

Juan Perón's ascent to power in Argentina was propelled by a combination of charisma, political acumen, and populist appeal. Perón, a former army officer, emerged as a champion of the working class and the dispossessed, promising to address their grievances and advance their interests. He capitalized on widespread discontent with the ruling oligarchy and the traditional political elites, tapping into a groundswell of support among urban workers, rural peasants, and marginalized sectors of society.

In 1946, Perón won a landslide victory in Argentina's presidential election, riding a wave of populist fervor and support from his loyal base of supporters, known as "Peronistas." His election marked a seismic shift in Argentine politics, as Perón became the country's first populist president and embarked on an ambitious program of social and economic reform.

Perón's populist policies were characterized by a mix of nationalism, corporatism, and social welfare programs aimed at empowering the working class and consolidating his political base. He implemented labor reforms, including the establishment of a minimum wage, collective bargaining rights, and social security benefits, which endeared him to organized labor and cemented his support among urban workers.

Furthermore, Perón pursued an agenda of economic nationalism, nationalizing key industries, and implementing protectionist measures to promote domestic industry and reduce dependence on foreign capital. His policies were hailed as a victory for Argentine sovereignty and economic independence, as he sought to break the country's historic reliance on foreign investment and influence.

The Role of Eva Perón in Peronist Argentina

Eva Perón, or "Evita" as she was affectionately known, played a pivotal role in shaping Peronist Argentina and cementing her husband's legacy as a champion of social justice and equality. As First Lady of Argentina, Evita emerged as a larger-than-life figure, renowned for her charisma, compassion, and tireless advocacy on behalf of the poor and marginalized.

Evita's influence extended far beyond the realm of traditional First Lady duties, as she spearheaded a wide range of social welfare programs and charitable initiatives aimed at improving the lives of the less fortunate. She established the

Eva Perón Foundation, which provided housing, healthcare, and education to the country's most vulnerable citizens, earning her widespread adulation and devotion from the Argentine people.

Moreover, Evita played a crucial role in mobilizing support for Perón and the Peronist movement, serving as a powerful orator and political organizer. Her impassioned speeches and public appearances galvanized support among Peronist supporters, while her tireless advocacy for women's rights and social justice helped to broaden the base of the Peronist movement and solidify its grip on power.

However, Evita's prominent role in Argentine politics also attracted controversy and criticism, as her extravagant lifestyle and growing influence sparked resentment among the country's traditional elites and conservative forces. Despite her popularity among the masses, Evita's political ambitions were ultimately thwarted by her untimely death from cancer in 1952, leaving a void in Argentine politics and society that would be deeply felt for years to come.

Legacy of Perónism in Argentine Politics

The legacy of Perónism in Argentine politics is complex and multifaceted, reflecting the enduring impact of Juan Perón and his populist movement on the country's political culture and identity. While Perón's rule was marked by authoritarianism, repression, and censorship, his legacy also includes significant achievements in the realms of social welfare, economic development, and national sovereignty.

Perónism has left an indelible mark on Argentine society, shaping the country's political landscape and influencing subsequent generations of leaders and political movements. Despite periodic setbacks and challenges, the Peronist movement has remained a dominant force in Argentine politics, evolving and adapting to changing circumstances while maintaining its core principles of social justice, economic nationalism, and solidarity.

Moreover, Peronism continues to inspire fervent loyalty and devotion among its supporters, who view it as a bulwark against neoliberalism, imperialism, and social inequality. The Peronist movement has proven resilient in the face of adversity, surviving periods of exile, repression, and internal divisions to emerge as a potent political force in Argentine politics.

However, Peronism's legacy is also fraught with contradictions and controversies, as its authoritarian tendencies and cult of personality have sparked fierce debate and division within Argentine society. The movement's legacy of political patronage, corruption, and cronyism has fueled skepticism and disillusionment among many Argentines, who view Peronism as a source of both promise and peril.

In conclusion, the era of Peronism in Argentina represents a complex and contested chapter in the country's history, marked by the rise of Juan Perón and the enduring legacy of his populist movement. While Peronism has left an indelible mark on Argentine politics and society, its legacy is a source of both inspiration and controversy, reflecting the enduring tensions between democracy and authoritarianism, nationalism and internationalism, and social justice and inequality in Argentine society.

Chapter 7: The Somoza Dynasty: Nicaragua, 1936-1979

The Somoza dynasty in Nicaragua represents one of the most enduring and oppressive dictatorships in Latin American history. Spanning from 1936 to 1979, the era of the Somoza regime was characterized by the establishment of a family dictatorship under Anastasio Somoza García, widespread repression and corruption, and ultimately, the dramatic fall of the Somoza dynasty at the hands of the Sandinista revolution. This chapter delves into the rise of Anastasio Somoza García and the consolidation of the Somoza family's grip on power, the pervasive repression and corruption that defined the Somoza regime, and the revolutionary upheaval that ultimately brought an end to their rule.

Anastasio Somoza García's Establishment of a Family Dictatorship

Anastasio Somoza García, a career military officer, rose to power in Nicaragua in 1936 following the assassination of General Augusto César Sandino, the leader of the Nicaraguan resistance movement against U.S. occupation. Somoza seized control of the National Guard, the country's main military force, and orchestrated a coup d'état, overthrowing the elected government and establishing himself as the de facto ruler of Nicaragua.

With the backing of the United States, Somoza consolidated power and established a family dictatorship that would endure for more than four decades. He created a political dynasty by installing family members and loyal allies in key positions of power, including his brothers Luis and Anastasio Jr., who succeeded him as president of Nicaragua in subsequent years.

Under Somoza's rule, Nicaragua became a virtual fiefdom controlled by the Somoza family and their cronies, as they amassed immense wealth and power at the expense of the Nicaraguan people. The National Guard served as the regime's enforcers, suppressing dissent and maintaining the Somoza's iron grip on power through a combination of violence, intimidation, and patronage.

Repression and Corruption Under the Somoza Regime

The Somoza regime was characterized by pervasive repression, censorship, and human rights abuses, as the regime sought to silence dissent and maintain its hold on power. Political opponents, labor activists, and social reformers were systematically targeted for harassment, imprisonment, and assassination, as the regime used terror and intimidation to crush any challenge to its authority.

Moreover, the Somoza family and their allies enriched themselves through corruption and cronyism, siphoning off millions of dollars in foreign aid and international loans meant for development projects and social welfare programs. State institutions were hollowed out and co-opted by the regime, as the judiciary, legislature, and civil service became tools of Somoza's personal enrichment and political control.

The regime's repression and corruption fueled widespread discontent and resistance among the Nicaraguan people, as growing social inequalities and economic injustices sparked calls for reform and revolution. However, dissent was met with brutal repression, as the regime's security forces cracked down on protests and demonstrations with impunity.

Sandinista Revolution and the Fall of the Somoza Dynasty

The Sandinista revolution, named after Augusto César Sandino, the revered nationalist hero, emerged as the vanguard of resistance against the Somoza regime in the 1960s and 1970s. The Sandinistas, a coalition of leftist guerrilla groups, labor unions, and student organizations, waged a protracted armed struggle against the Somoza dictatorship, seeking to overthrow the regime and establish a socialist government based on principles of social justice and national sovereignty.

The Sandinista revolution gained momentum in the 1970s, fueled by growing popular discontent and international support for their cause. The regime's brutality and corruption had alienated key sectors of Nicaraguan society, including the peasantry, the urban poor, and the middle class, who rallied behind the Sandinista movement in their quest for freedom and justice.

In 1978, the assassination of prominent journalist Pedro Joaquín Chamorro sparked widespread protests and demonstrations against the regime, leading to a nationwide uprising against the Somoza dictatorship. The Sandinistas, leading a coalition of opposition forces, launched a final offensive against the regime's stronghold in Managua, the capital city, culminating in the overthrow of Anastasio Somoza Debayle, the son of Anastasio Somoza García, in July 1979.

Conclusion

The fall of the Somoza dynasty in Nicaragua marked the end of one of the most oppressive and corrupt dictatorships in Latin American history and the dawn of a new era of hope and transformation for the Nicaraguan people. The Sandinista revolution, inspired by the legacy of Augusto César Sandino and fueled by the courage and determination of the Nicaraguan people, succeeded in overthrowing the Somoza regime and ushering in a period of revolutionary change and social progress.

However, the legacy of the Somoza dynasty continues to cast a long shadow over Nicaragua, as the country grapples with the legacy of dictatorship, repression, and corruption. The wounds of the past are still raw for many Nicaraguans, as they seek to rebuild their country and forge a path towards democracy, justice, and reconciliation.

In examining the rise and fall of the Somoza dynasty, we gain valuable insights into the complex dynamics of power, corruption, and resistance that have shaped Nicaraguan history and identity. Moving forward, it is essential to confront the legacies of dictatorship and authoritarianism, fostering a culture of democracy, human rights, and accountability that honors the memory of those who suffered under the yoke of tyranny.

Chapter 8: The Batista Regime: Cuba, 1952-1959

The Batista regime in Cuba, spanning from 1952 to 1959, represents a tumultuous period in Cuban history marked by dictatorship, corruption, and the seeds of revolution. This chapter explores Fulgencio Batista's return to power through a coup, the pervasive corruption and ties with organized crime that characterized his regime, and the rise of Fidel Castro and the Cuban Revolution that ultimately brought an end to Batista's rule.

Fulgencio Batista's Return to Power Through a Coup

Fulgencio Batista's return to power in Cuba in 1952 marked a significant turning point in the country's history. After serving as president from 1940 to 1944, Batista had relinquished power and gone into exile, only to return in 1952 and seize control of the government in a military coup. With the backing of the Cuban armed forces and support from wealthy business interests, Batista suspended the constitution, dissolved the legislature, and established himself as the de facto ruler of Cuba.

Batista's return to power represented a betrayal of Cuba's democratic ideals and a consolidation of authoritarian rule. Under his regime, civil liberties were curtailed, political opposition was suppressed, and dissent was met with violence and intimidation. Batista ruled with an iron fist, using the military and secret police to crush any challenge to his authority and maintain his grip on power.

Dictatorship, Corruption, and Ties with Organized Crime

The Batista regime was characterized by pervasive corruption, cronyism, and ties with organized crime, as Batista and his associates enriched themselves at the expense of the Cuban people. Under Batista's rule, Cuba became a playground for mobsters, gangsters, and corrupt politicians, as gambling, prostitution, and drug trafficking flourished under the protection of the regime.

Batista and his cronies amassed immense wealth through kickbacks, bribes, and embezzlement, siphoning off millions of dollars in public funds meant for development projects and social welfare programs. State institutions were hollowed out and co-opted by the regime, as the judiciary, legislature, and civil service became tools of Batista's personal enrichment and political control.

Moreover, the regime's ties with organized crime further eroded the rule of law and undermined public trust in government institutions. Batista turned a blind eye to the activities of the mafia and other criminal syndicates, allowing them to operate with impunity in exchange for their support and financial contributions to his regime. The resulting culture of corruption and lawlessness fueled widespread discontent and resentment among the Cuban people, laying the groundwork for the revolutionary upheaval that would ultimately bring an end to Batista's rule.

Rise of Fidel Castro and the Cuban Revolution

The rise of Fidel Castro and the Cuban Revolution emerged as a response to the oppressive and corrupt regime of Fulgencio Batista. Fidel Castro, a charismatic young lawyer and political activist, emerged as the leader of the revolutionary movement, rallying support among students, workers, and peasants who were disillusioned with Batista's dictatorship.

Castro's revolutionary message of social justice, economic equality, and national sovereignty struck a chord with the Cuban people, as he promised to overthrow the corrupt and repressive regime of Batista and establish a government based on principles of democracy and socialism. In 1956, Castro and a small band of guerrilla fighters launched a rebellion against the Batista regime, beginning a protracted armed struggle that would ultimately lead to the downfall of Batista's rule.

The Cuban Revolution gained momentum in the late 1950s, fueled by growing popular discontent and international support for Castro's cause. Batista's brutal repression of dissent only served to galvanize support for the revolution, as the regime's human rights abuses and ties with organized crime sparked outrage and condemnation both at home and abroad.

In January 1959, Castro and his rebel forces finally succeeded in overthrowing Batista's regime, forcing the dictator to flee the country and go into exile. The Cuban Revolution marked the beginning of a new era in Cuban history, as Castro and his allies set about implementing sweeping social, economic, and political reforms aimed at transforming Cuban society and building a socialist future.

Conclusion

The Batista regime in Cuba represents a dark chapter in the country's history, marked by dictatorship, corruption, and ties with organized crime. Fulgencio Batista's return to power through a military coup represented a betrayal of Cuba's democratic ideals and a consolidation of authoritarian rule. Under his regime, Cuba became a playground for mobsters and corrupt politicians, as state institutions were hollowed out and co-opted by the regime for personal enrichment and political control.

However, the rise of Fidel Castro and the Cuban Revolution ultimately brought an end to Batista's rule and ushered in a period of radical transformation and social change. Castro's revolutionary message of social justice and national sovereignty resonated with the Cuban people, as they rallied behind his cause in their quest for freedom and equality.

In examining the rise and fall of the Batista regime, we gain valuable insights into the complex dynamics of power, corruption, and resistance that have shaped Cuban history and identity. Moving forward, it is essential to confront the legacies of dictatorship and authoritarianism, fostering a culture of democracy, human rights, and accountability that honors the memory of those who suffered under the yoke of tyranny.

Chapter 9: The Pinochet Era: Chile, 1973-1990

The Pinochet era in Chile, spanning from 1973 to 1990, represents a period of profound political upheaval, repression, and transformation. This chapter explores the rise of Salvador Allende to the presidency and the subsequent coup d'état in 1973, the military dictatorship under Augusto Pinochet, the widespread human rights violations and economic policies implemented during the regime, and the transition to democracy that marked the end of Pinochet's rule.

Salvador Allende's Presidency and the 1973 Coup d'État

Salvador Allende, a socialist and leader of the Popular Unity coalition, was elected president of Chile in 1970, marking the first time in Latin America that a Marxist had been democratically elected to the highest office. Allende's presidency represented a radical departure from Chile's traditional political establishment, as he pursued an ambitious program of social and economic reform aimed at reducing poverty, inequality, and dependence on foreign capital.

However, Allende's socialist policies quickly sparked controversy and resistance from conservative forces within Chile, as well as from the United States government, which viewed Allende's government as a threat to its interests in the region. The CIA, in collaboration with elements within the Chilean military and business elite, orchestrated a campaign of destabilization and sabotage aimed at undermining Allende's government and fomenting a coup.

On September 11, 1973, the Chilean military, led by General Augusto Pinochet, launched a violent coup d'état, overthrowing Allende's government and installing a military junta in its place. Allende died under mysterious circumstances during the coup, with the official narrative stating that he committed suicide, although some believe he was killed by military forces.

Military Dictatorship under Augusto Pinochet

The coup d'état of 1973 ushered in a brutal military dictatorship under Augusto Pinochet, who would rule Chile with an iron fist for the next 17 years. Pinochet, a staunch anti-communist and admirer of authoritarian regimes, quickly consolidated power and established a regime characterized by repression, censorship, and human rights abuses.

Under Pinochet's rule, Chilean society was subjected to widespread repression and violence, as political opponents, labor activists, and perceived enemies of the regime were systematically targeted for arrest, torture, and assassination. The regime's security forces, including the infamous Directorate of National Intelligence (DINA), operated with impunity, terrorizing the population and suppressing dissent through a combination of intimidation and brutality.

Moreover, Pinochet's regime implemented a policy of neoliberal economic reforms, privatizing state-owned enterprises, deregulating the economy, and implementing austerity measures aimed at reducing inflation and stimulating growth. While these policies succeeded in stabilizing the economy and attracting foreign investment, they also exacerbated social inequalities and deepened poverty, as public services were slashed and workers' rights were eroded.

Human Rights Violations, Economic Policies, and the Transition to Democracy

The Pinochet regime's human rights violations, economic policies, and repressive tactics sparked widespread condemnation and resistance both within Chile and internationally. Human rights organizations documented thousands of cases of torture, disappearance, and extrajudicial killing committed by the regime's security forces, leading to calls for accountability and justice.

Despite the regime's efforts to suppress dissent and maintain its grip on power, opposition to Pinochet's dictatorship continued to grow, fueled by a broad coalition of political parties, labor unions, and civil society organizations. In 1988, under mounting pressure from domestic and international actors, Pinochet agreed to hold a national referendum on his continued rule, which ultimately resulted in his defeat and the initiation of a transition to democracy.

In 1990, Pinochet stepped down from power and Chile held its first democratic elections in nearly two decades, marking the end of the Pinochet era and the beginning of a new chapter in Chilean history. However, the legacy of Pinochet's dictatorship continues to loom large in Chilean society, as the country grapples with the legacy of repression, trauma, and political polarization that characterized the Pinochet era.

Conclusion

The Pinochet era in Chile represents a dark and tumultuous chapter in the country's history, marked by dictatorship, repression, and economic transformation. Salvador Allende's presidency and the subsequent coup d'état of 1973 led to the establishment of a brutal military dictatorship under Augusto Pinochet, characterized by widespread human rights violations, neoliberal economic policies, and authoritarian rule.

However, the Pinochet era also galvanized resistance and resilience among the Chilean people, as they fought tirelessly for democracy, justice, and human rights. The transition to democracy in 1990 marked the end of Pinochet's rule and the beginning of a new era of hope and reconciliation for Chile, as the country embarked on a path towards healing and democratic renewal.

In examining the Pinochet era, we gain valuable insights into the complexities of power, repression, and resistance that have shaped Chilean society and politics. Moving forward, it is essential to confront the legacies of dictatorship and authoritarianism, fostering a culture of democracy, human rights, and social justice that honors the memory of those who suffered under the yoke of tyranny.

Chapter 10: The Dirty War in Argentina: 1976-1983

The Dirty War in Argentina, spanning from 1976 to 1983, stands as one of the darkest periods in the country's history. This chapter delves into the military coup that led to the establishment of the junta, the state terrorism, forced disappearances, and torture inflicted upon dissenters, and the courageous struggle for justice led by the Mothers of the Plaza de Mayo.

Military Coup and the Establishment of the Junta

On March 24, 1976, a military junta led by General Jorge Rafael Videla seized power in Argentina, overthrowing the democratically elected government of President Isabel Perón. The coup marked the culmination of years of political instability, economic turmoil, and social unrest, as right-wing military factions sought to restore order and combat what they perceived as a growing threat of communism and subversion.

The military junta, composed of army, navy, and air force commanders, immediately implemented a brutal campaign of repression and state terrorism aimed at eliminating perceived enemies of the regime and restoring "order" to Argentine society. Under the pretext of combating terrorism and subversion, the junta launched a ruthless crackdown on political dissent, labor activism, and social movements, targeting leftist guerrilla groups, labor unions, student organizations, and anyone deemed a threat to the regime's authority.

State Terrorism, Forced Disappearances, and Torture

The Dirty War in Argentina was characterized by widespread human rights violations, including forced disappearances, extrajudicial killings, and torture. The regime's security forces, including the infamous intelligence agency known as the National Reorganization Process (PRT), operated with impunity, carrying out systematic acts of violence and repression against perceived enemies of the state.

Thousands of individuals, including students, intellectuals, activists, and suspected members of leftist organizations, were abducted by security forces and taken to secret detention centers, where they were interrogated, tortured, and often killed. The regime's use of forced disappearances, a tactic designed to instill fear and silence dissent, left families and communities devastated, as they struggled to find out the fate of their loved ones.

Torture was widespread in Argentina's clandestine detention centers, where prisoners were subjected to brutal interrogation techniques, including beatings, electric shocks, waterboarding, and sexual violence. The regime's use of torture was not only intended to extract information and confessions but also to intimidate and terrorize the population into submission.

Mothers of the Plaza de Mayo and the Struggle for Justice

Amidst the reign of terror unleashed by the military junta, a courageous group of women emerged as symbols of resistance and resilience in the face of adversity. The Mothers of the Plaza de Mayo, led by women like Hebe de Bonafini and Azucena Villaflor, began gathering in the Plaza de Mayo in Buenos Aires, demanding information about the fate of their disappeared children and denouncing the regime's atrocities.

The Mothers of the Plaza de Mayo transformed their grief and anguish into a powerful political movement, demanding accountability for the crimes committed by the regime and seeking justice for the victims of forced disappearances and state terrorism. Despite facing threats, harassment, and intimidation from the regime's security forces, the Mothers persisted in their struggle, refusing to be silenced or intimidated.

Their activism, along with the efforts of human rights organizations and international pressure, played a crucial role in exposing the truth about the Dirty War and holding the perpetrators accountable for their crimes. In the years following the end of military rule, Argentina's democratic government took steps to prosecute those responsible for human rights violations, leading to the trials and convictions of several high-ranking military officers.

Conclusion

The Dirty War in Argentina represents a dark and painful chapter in the country's history, marked by state terrorism, forced disappearances, and widespread human rights violations. The military junta's reign of terror inflicted untold suffering and devastation upon Argentine society, leaving scars that continue to linger to this day.

However, amidst the horror and despair, the courage and resilience of individuals like the Mothers of the Plaza de Mayo serve as a beacon of hope and inspiration. Their relentless pursuit of truth, justice, and accountability has helped to shine a light on the atrocities committed during the Dirty War and ensure that the memory of the victims is not forgotten.

In examining the Dirty War in Argentina, we gain valuable insights into the complexities of power, violence, and resistance that have shaped Argentine society and politics. Moving forward, it is essential to confront the legacies of dictatorship and authoritarianism, fostering a culture of democracy, human rights, and social justice that honors the memory of those who suffered and sacrifices of those who fought for freedom and dignity.

Chapter 11: The Noriega Regime: Panama, 1983-1989

The Noriega regime in Panama, spanning from 1983 to 1989, represents a turbulent period in Panamanian history characterized by dictatorship, drug trafficking, corruption, and ultimately, intervention by the United States. This chapter explores Manuel Noriega's rise to power and his ties with the United States, the pervasive drug trafficking, corruption, and human rights abuses that defined his regime, and the U.S. invasion of Panama that led to the end of Noriega's rule.

Manuel Noriega's Rise to Power and Ties with the United States

Manuel Antonio Noriega, a career military officer, rose to power in Panama in the 1980s, emerging as one of the country's most powerful and influential figures. Noriega initially rose through the ranks of the Panamanian military, cultivating close ties with the United States and serving as a key ally in the region during the Cold War.

Throughout the 1970s and 1980s, Noriega worked closely with U.S. intelligence agencies, providing valuable intelligence on leftist movements in Latin America and facilitating covert operations in the region. However, Noriega's relationship with the United States became increasingly complicated as allegations of corruption, drug trafficking, and human rights abuses began to surface.

Despite growing concerns about Noriega's conduct, the United States continued to support his regime, viewing him as a strategic ally in the fight against communism and leftist movements in Latin America. However, tensions between Noriega and the United States escalated in the late 1980s, as evidence of his involvement in drug trafficking and other illicit activities became impossible to ignore.

Drug Trafficking, Corruption, and Human Rights Abuses

The Noriega regime in Panama was characterized by widespread corruption, drug trafficking, and human rights abuses, as Noriega and his associates enriched themselves at the expense of the Panamanian people. Under Noriega's rule, Panama became a major hub for drug trafficking, as the regime colluded with Colombian drug cartels and facilitated the transit of narcotics through Panamanian territory.

Moreover, Noriega and his inner circle amassed immense wealth through embezzlement, bribery, and extortion, siphoning off millions of dollars in public funds and international aid meant for development projects and social welfare programs. State institutions were hollowed out and co-opted by the regime, as the judiciary, legislature, and civil service became tools of Noriega's personal enrichment and political control.

The Noriega regime also engaged in widespread human rights abuses, including extrajudicial killings, torture, and repression of political dissent. Opposition leaders, journalists, and activists were targeted for harassment, imprisonment, and assassination, as the regime sought to silence any challenge to its authority.

U.S. Invasion and the End of Noriega's Regime

Tensions between Noriega and the United States came to a head in December 1989, when Noriega's regime was accused of rigging the presidential election in Panama. In response, the United States launched Operation Just Cause, a military invasion of Panama aimed at overthrowing Noriega and restoring democracy to the country.

The U.S. invasion of Panama, which began on December 20, 1989, marked the first time since the Vietnam War that the United States had deployed troops in a foreign country for the purpose of regime change. The invasion was swift and decisive, as U.S. forces quickly overwhelmed the Panamanian military and captured Noriega, who was subsequently extradited to the United States to stand trial on drug trafficking charges.

The U.S. invasion of Panama led to the collapse of the Noriega regime and the establishment of a civilian government in Panama. However, the invasion also resulted in significant loss of life and widespread destruction, as civilian neighborhoods were bombed and innocent civilians caught in the crossfire.

Conclusion

The Noriega regime in Panama represents a dark and tumultuous chapter in the country's history, marked by dictatorship, drug trafficking, corruption, and human rights abuses. Manuel Noriega's rise to power and his ties with the United States illustrate the complexities of geopolitics and the consequences of supporting authoritarian regimes in pursuit of strategic interests.

The U.S. invasion of Panama, while ostensibly aimed at restoring democracy and ending Noriega's reign of terror, also raises questions about the use of military force and the broader implications of intervention in the affairs of sovereign nations. The invasion led to the collapse of the Noriega regime, but it also resulted in significant loss of life and destruction, leaving scars that continue to linger in Panama to this day.

In examining the Noriega regime in Panama, we gain valuable insights into the complexities of power, corruption, and resistance that have shaped Panamanian society and politics. Moving forward, it is essential to confront the legacies of dictatorship and authoritarianism, fostering a culture of democracy, human rights, and accountability that honors the memory of those who suffered under the yoke of tyranny.

Chapter 12: Fujimori's Peru: 1990-2000

The decade of Alberto Fujimori's presidency in Peru, from 1990 to 2000, stands as a complex and controversial period in the country's history. This chapter explores Fujimori's rise to power and his establishment of authoritarian governance, the economic reforms and human rights violations that marked his tenure, and the events leading to Fujimori's downfall and his lasting legacy in Peruvian politics.

Alberto Fujimori's Presidency and Authoritarian Governance

Alberto Fujimori, a little-known agricultural engineer of Japanese descent, emerged as an unlikely candidate in Peru's presidential elections in 1990. Running on a platform of populist reform and anti-corruption, Fujimori won a surprise victory, defeating the renowned novelist Mario Vargas Llosa.

Once in office, Fujimori quickly consolidated power and established an authoritarian regime characterized by the concentration of power in the executive branch and the erosion of democratic institutions. Fujimori dissolved Congress and the judiciary, assuming near-dictatorial powers and ruling by decree through the use of emergency legislation.

Fujimori's presidency was marked by a cult of personality, as he portrayed himself as a strong and decisive leader capable of restoring order and stability to a country plagued by economic crisis, political turmoil, and internal conflict. However, his authoritarian governance would ultimately lead to widespread human rights violations and the erosion of civil liberties.

Economic Reforms, Human Rights Violations, and the Fight Against Terrorism

Fujimori's presidency was also characterized by a series of neoliberal economic reforms aimed at stabilizing the economy and attracting foreign investment. Fujimori implemented austerity measures, privatized state-owned enterprises, and deregulated the economy, leading to economic growth and macroeconomic stability.

However, these economic reforms came at a heavy cost, as they exacerbated social inequalities and deepened poverty, particularly in rural and indigenous communities. Fujimori's policies led to widespread social unrest and protests, as workers, peasants, and students took to the streets to demand social justice and economic equality.

Moreover, Fujimori's regime was responsible for egregious human rights violations, including extrajudicial killings, forced disappearances, and torture. The regime's security forces, including the infamous Grupo Colina death squad, targeted suspected members of leftist guerrilla groups, labor activists, and political opponents, using terror and intimidation to silence dissent and maintain control.

Fujimori justified these human rights abuses as necessary measures in the fight against terrorism, particularly against the Shining Path guerrilla movement, which had launched a brutal insurgency aimed at overthrowing the government and establishing a communist state. However, the regime's tactics of repression and violence only served to further polarize Peruvian society and fuel the cycle of violence.

Fujimori's Downfall and Legacy in Peruvian Politics

Fujimori's downfall came in 2000, amid mounting allegations of corruption and electoral fraud. Facing growing opposition and international pressure, Fujimori fled to Japan, where he attempted to govern from exile before being extradited to Peru to stand trial on charges of human rights abuses and corruption.

Fujimori's legacy in Peruvian politics remains deeply controversial and divisive. While some view him as a strong and decisive leader who brought stability and economic growth to Peru, others condemn him as an authoritarian dictator who trampled on democracy and human rights in pursuit of power.

Despite his imprisonment and disgrace, Fujimori's influence continues to loom large in Peruvian politics, as his daughter Keiko Fujimori has emerged as a prominent political figure and leader of the right-wing populist movement in Peru. The legacy of Fujimori's presidency serves as a cautionary tale about the dangers of authoritarianism and the importance of upholding democratic values and institutions.

Conclusion

The decade of Alberto Fujimori's presidency in Peru represents a complex and controversial period in the country's history, marked by authoritarian governance, economic reforms, human rights violations, and the fight against terrorism. Fujimori's rise to power and his establishment of an authoritarian regime have left a lasting impact on Peruvian politics, shaping the country's political landscape and identity in profound ways.

In examining Fujimori's presidency, we gain valuable insights into the complexities of power, corruption, and resistance that have shaped Peruvian society and politics. Moving forward, it is essential to confront the legacies of dictatorship and authoritarianism, fostering a culture of democracy, human rights, and accountability that honors the memory of those who suffered under the yoke of tyranny.

Chapter 13: The Legacy of Authoritarianism

Authoritarian regimes have left a profound and lasting impact on the countries they ruled, shaping societies, economies, and political cultures in complex and enduring ways. This chapter conducts a comparative analysis of the dictatorships discussed in this book, highlighting their commonalities and differences, and examines the impact of authoritarianism on society, the economy, and political culture. Furthermore, it explores the challenges of democratic transition and the persistence of authoritarian legacies in the post-dictatorship era.

Comparative Analysis of the Dictatorships: Commonalities and Differences

Across 20th-century Latin America, authoritarian regimes shared certain commonalities in their methods of governance and strategies for maintaining power. These included the concentration of power in the hands of a single leader or ruling clique, the suppression of political opposition and dissent, the use of state violence and repression to silence critics, and the manipulation of state institutions to serve the interests of the ruling elite.

However, there were also significant differences among the dictatorships in terms of their ideological orientation, socioeconomic context, and methods of rule. For example, some regimes, such as those of Juan Perón in Argentina and Getúlio

Vargas in Brazil, embraced populist policies aimed at mobilizing popular support and co-opting social movements, while others, such as those of Rafael Trujillo in the Dominican Republic and Augusto Pinochet in Chile, relied on authoritarian rule and state terror to maintain control.

Impact on Society, Economy, and Political Culture

Authoritarian regimes had a profound impact on the societies they ruled, leaving behind a legacy of repression, fear, and trauma. The widespread human rights abuses, censorship, and state violence inflicted by these regimes left deep scars on the collective memory of their societies, contributing to a culture of fear and distrust that continues to linger long after the dictatorships have ended.

Moreover, authoritarian rule often stifled political participation and civil society activism, undermining democratic values and institutions and perpetuating a culture of apathy and resignation among the population. Economic policies implemented by authoritarian regimes, such as neoliberal reforms and state-led development strategies, had mixed results, leading to economic growth and modernization in some cases, but also exacerbating social inequalities and deepening poverty in others.

Challenges of Democratic Transition and the Persistence of Authoritarian Legacies

The transition from authoritarian rule to democracy has posed significant challenges for countries grappling with the legacy of dictatorship. While the overthrow of authoritarian regimes represents a victory for democracy and human rights, the transition process is often fraught with obstacles, including resistance from entrenched elites, weak institutions, and the persistence of authoritarian legacies.

In many cases, the transition to democracy has been incomplete, as former regime officials and military leaders retain significant power and influence in the post-dictatorship era. Moreover, the legacies of authoritarianism, including corruption, impunity, and social polarization, continue to shape political dynamics and hinder democratic consolidation in countries emerging from dictatorship.

Conclusion

The legacy of authoritarianism in 20th-century Latin America is complex and multifaceted, encompassing a range of political, economic, and social factors that continue to shape the region's trajectory to this day. While the dictatorships discussed in this book differed in their methods and ideologies, they shared certain commonalities in their use of repression, violence, and manipulation to maintain power.

Moving forward, it is essential for countries to confront the legacies of dictatorship and authoritarianism, fostering a culture of democracy, human rights, and accountability that honors the memory of those who suffered under the yoke of tyranny. This requires addressing the root causes of authoritarianism, promoting inclusive political participation, and strengthening democratic institutions to ensure that the mistakes of the past are not repeated. Only by confronting the legacy of authoritarianism can Latin America truly achieve a future of peace, prosperity, and democratic governance.

Chapter 14: Remembering the Victims

The victims of authoritarian regimes in 20th-century Latin America were countless, their lives disrupted or destroyed by oppression, violence, and injustice. This chapter delves into the stories of resistance, activism, and survival under dictatorship, explores the efforts to commemorate the victims and seek truth and justice, and underscores the importance of memory and reconciliation in post-dictatorship societies.

Stories of Resistance, Activism, and Survival under Dictatorship

Throughout the history of authoritarian rule in Latin America, individuals and communities resisted oppression and fought for justice, often at great personal risk. From political activists and human rights defenders to ordinary citizens who dared to speak out against injustice, the stories of resistance and survival under dictatorship are a testament to the resilience of the human spirit in the face of tyranny.

Many victims of dictatorship became symbols of resistance and courage, inspiring others to join the struggle for freedom and democracy. Their stories serve as a reminder of the power of solidarity and collective action in the face of adversity, as well as the importance of standing up for human rights and dignity in the darkest of times.

Commemoration Efforts and the Quest for

Truth and Justice

In the aftermath of dictatorship, societies across Latin America have embarked on efforts to commemorate the victims and seek truth and justice for the crimes committed during the authoritarian era. Truth commissions, memorial sites, and commemorative events have been established to honor the memory of those who suffered and to ensure that their stories are not forgotten.

Furthermore, legal mechanisms such as trials and prosecutions have been pursued to hold perpetrators accountable for their actions and provide a measure of justice for the victims and their families. These efforts to confront the past and reckon with the legacy of dictatorship are essential for healing the wounds of history and building a more just and democratic future.

Importance of Memory and Reconciliation in Post-Dictatorship Societies

Memory and reconciliation play a crucial role in post-dictatorship societies, providing a foundation for healing, reconciliation, and democratic renewal. By acknowledging the suffering and injustices of the past, societies can begin the process of healing and reconciliation, fostering a culture of empathy, solidarity, and mutual respect.

Moreover, remembering the victims of dictatorship is essential for safeguarding democracy and human rights in the future, as it serves as a reminder of the dangers of authoritarianism and the importance of vigilance in defending democratic values and institutions. By learning from the mistakes of the past, societies can build a more inclusive, equitable, and democratic future for all.

Conclusion

The victims of authoritarian regimes in 20th-century Latin America were ordinary people who found themselves caught up in the tumult of history, their lives forever altered by the cruelty and injustice of dictatorship. Their stories of resistance, activism, and survival serve as a powerful reminder of the resilience of the human spirit and the enduring quest for freedom and justice.

As societies grapple with the legacy of dictatorship, it is essential to remember the victims and honor their memory through commemoration efforts and the pursuit of truth and justice. By confronting the past and reckoning with the wounds of history, societies can begin the process of healing and reconciliation, forging a path towards a more just, democratic, and peaceful future for all.

Chapter 15: Conclusion

As we conclude our exploration of authoritarian regimes in 20th-century Latin America, it is important to reflect on the lessons learned, the challenges faced, and the prospects for democracy in the region. This final chapter provides a synthesis of our study, examining the enduring legacy of dictatorship in the 21st century and offering insights into the path forward for Latin American societies.

Reflections on the Study of Authoritarian Regimes in Latin America

The study of authoritarian regimes in Latin America offers valuable insights into the complexities of power, politics, and society in the region. By examining the rise and fall of dictatorships, we gain a deeper understanding of the factors that contribute to authoritarianism, including social inequality, political instability, and external intervention.

Moreover, the study of authoritarianism in Latin America highlights the resilience of the human spirit in the face of oppression and injustice. From stories of resistance and activism to efforts to commemorate the victims and seek truth and justice, the history of dictatorship in the region is marked by acts of courage, solidarity, and perseverance.

Lessons Learned and Prospects for Democracy

One of the key lessons learned from the study of authoritarian regimes in Latin America is the importance of defending democratic values and institutions in the face of tyranny. Democracy is not a given but rather a constant struggle that requires vigilance, participation, and commitment from all members of society.

Moreover, the experience of dictatorship underscores the need for inclusive, equitable, and accountable governance that addresses the root causes of social and political instability. By addressing issues such as poverty, inequality, and corruption, societies can build a more resilient and sustainable democracy that is responsive to the needs and aspirations of all citizens.

The Enduring Legacy of Dictatorship in the 21st Century

Despite the transition to democracy in many countries in Latin America, the legacy of dictatorship continues to cast a long shadow over the region. Authoritarian legacies, including corruption, impunity, and social polarization, persist in post-dictatorship societies, posing challenges to democratic governance and stability.

Moreover, the rise of populist leaders and authoritarian tendencies in the 21st century underscores the fragility of democracy in Latin America and the need for constant vigilance in defending democratic values and institutions. By learning from the mistakes of the past and confronting the legacies of dictatorship, societies can build a more resilient and inclusive democracy for the future.

Conclusion

In conclusion, the study of authoritarian regimes in Latin America offers valuable insights into the complexities of power, politics, and society in the region. By reflecting on the lessons learned from the history of dictatorship, we can better understand the challenges faced and the prospects for democracy in the 21st century.

Moving forward, it is essential for Latin American societies to confront the legacies of dictatorship, defend democratic values and institutions, and build a more inclusive and equitable future for all. By working together to address the root causes of social and political instability, we can build a more resilient and sustainable democracy that reflects the aspirations and values of the people of Latin America.

Don't miss out!

Visit the website below and you can sign up to receive emails whenever MICHAEL SMITH publishes a new book. There's no charge and no obligation.

https://books2read.com/r/B-A-RBLKB-XMKHD

BOOKS 2 READ

Connecting independent readers to independent writers.

About the Author

Michael Smith, an American literature scholar, holds a Ph.D. in English Literature and teaches at the university level. With a focus on American literary tradition, Smith's engaging prose and scholarly insight have graced academic journals and literary magazines. He explores diverse voices and themes in American literature, from classics to contemporary works. Smith's passion for storytelling extends beyond academia, inspiring readers to appreciate the depth and complexity of American letters.

www.ingramcontent.com/pod-product-compliance
Lightning Source LLC
Chambersburg PA
CBHW051818130726
47987CB00003B/1315